D1710277

Now You See Me

Fulton Books, Inc.
Meadville, PA

Published by Fulton Books 2021

ISBN 978-1-63860-078-7 (paperback)
ISBN 978-1-63985-463-9 (hardcover)
ISBN 978-1-63860-079-4 (digital)

Printed in the United States of America

NOW YOU SEE ME

A Picture Book Written and Illustrated by

Declan Sarlson

My name is David (never Dave).
I'm ten.

I'm an Aspie. *Aspie* is short for Asperger's syndrome. At least that is what it used to be called. Now it is called ASD, which is short for "autism spectrum disorder." Whatever.

I may seem a little different to you than most kids.
That's okay, you're just noticing my special abilities.

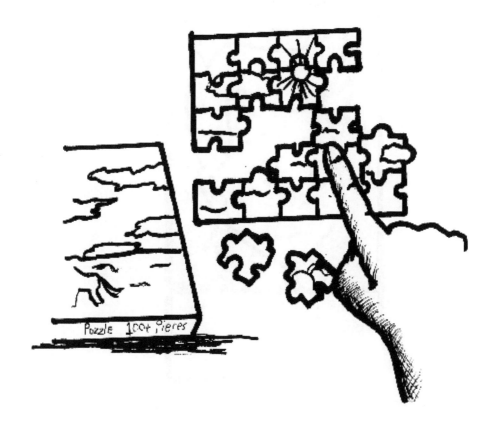

My parents call them my superpowers.

You may have seen me pacing at the back
of the classroom or in the hallway.

Sometimes I get anxious about things, and this repetitive motion helps me figure things out.

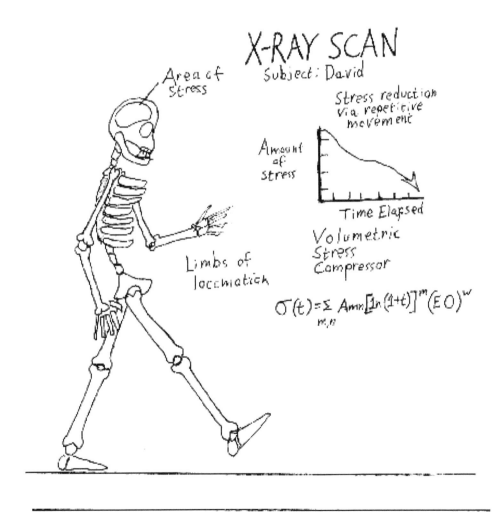

You may have seen me get picked on or teased by other kids at school. They don't understand that my brain is just wired a little differently.

You may have seen me by myself in the lunchroom or on the bus. I bet you don't think it is possible to be alone in a room full of people, but you can.

Sometimes the lunchroom is too loud. I have to leave.

You may have seen me sitting by myself at my desk at lunchtime instead. I can think much better when it is quiet.

You may have seen me getting anxious
during fireworks or in assemblies.

That may be because my hearing is enhanced.

I can hear through thin walls. Sometimes
I think I can hear ants fighting!

Riding home on the school bus is torture.

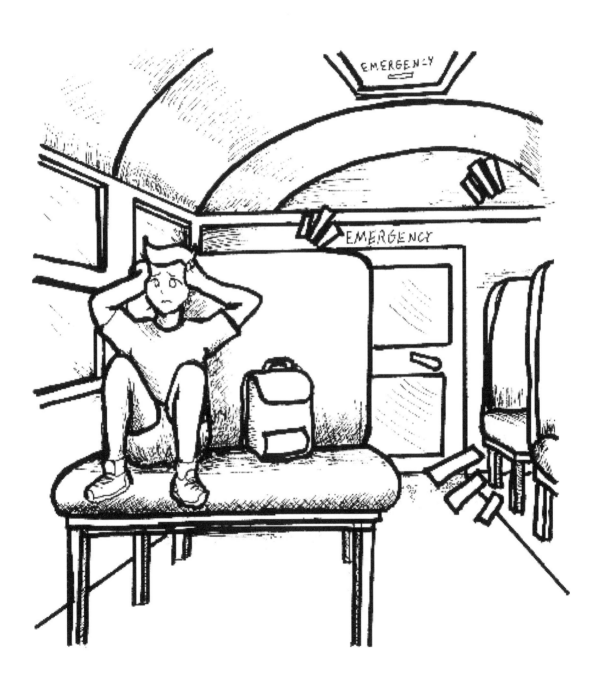

You may have gotten annoyed with me when you talked to me. Sometimes I don't look at you when you speak to me.

I'm listening. I just don't always remember to make eye contact.

If I don't know you or if I think you are going to make fun of me, I will probably let you do all of the talking.

Sometimes it is easier to be quiet.

You may have seen me hanging out with my grandpa a lot. I like Grandpa.

We tell great jokes and watch World War II movies. Grandpa is patient with me, and he likes me just the way I am.

I have been told I don't have a "filter," whatever that means.

When people ask me things, I tell them. Sometimes I forget that being honest can sound a little mean. I'm not mean. I just haven't really learned how to be honest more nicely.

Grandpa doesn't have a filter either.

Maybe that is why we get along.

You might have seen me walking around with
my notebook and pen. I like to draw—a lot.
My parents joke that my notebook and
pen are surgically attached to my arm.
I don't get it.

When I was really little, I couldn't express myself very well.

I used to get really angry and frustrated.

I got kicked out of one preschool after
another until I started drawing.

I began drawing cartoons when I was little
so I could say what I was feeling.

I create a lot of characters with my pen and notebook.

I create worlds where people don't get impatient with me.

You may have seen me look a little puzzled at jokes. Words with double meanings baffle me.

Sometimes I have a hard time understanding how word jokes are funny. I like slapstick though. Nothing says "funny" like a cream pie in the face!

I like having a plan for my day. I like knowing what I need to do and where I need to go.

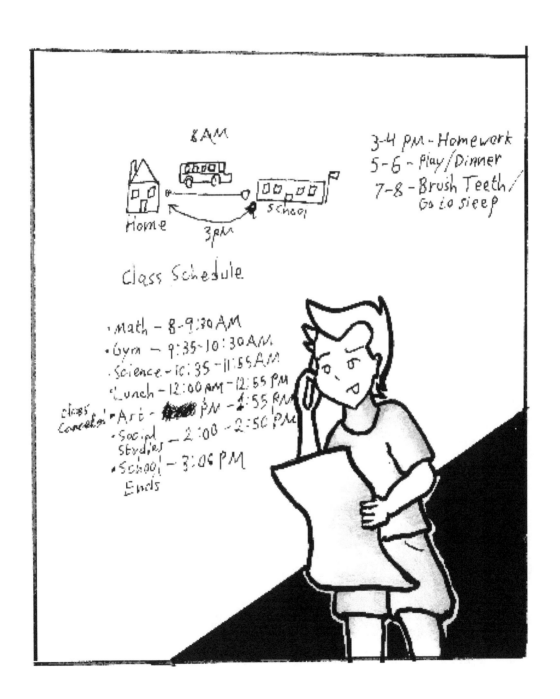

I really like having a checklist and checking
things off as I get them done.

I really don't handle surprises very well
unless they involve cake and candles.

And pizza.

You may have seen me in the puzzle corner at school.

I'm a wiz at spotting patterns.

In fact, I've been told that Aspies are 40 percent better at solving puzzles than non-Aspies. That's another superpower.

Next time you need a teammate for a puzzle challenge, I'm your man.

You may have seen me talking about the same topic time and time again. There are certain things that I find very interesting.

I can talk about them for hours. Sometimes they are so interesting that I really don't want to talk about anything else.

My parents call this my "monologue."

Grandpa just tells me to snap out of it.

You may have seen me as the quiet kid with few friends.

I hope that now you see me as I really am.
I have some pretty cool superpowers that
are going to come in handy someday.

You may see some other kid just like me.

Be nice to him. He's probably got a lot on his mind and doesn't know how to express it.

I'm pretty sure he needs a friend who is patient and will accept him just as he is.

I'm David. I'm an Aspie. Now you see me.

About the Author

Declan Sarlson is a senior at Ursuline College in Pepper Pike, Ohio. He is pursuing a degree in art and intends to build a career as a graphic novelist. Mr. Sarlson lives in Novelty, Ohio, with his family.

CPSIA information can be obtained
at www.ICGtesting.com
Printed in the USA
LVHW060929201221
706484LV00042B/691

9 781639 854639